MILLIE: BOOK TWO

THE BUTTON NECKLACE

TROON HARRISON

Millie: Book Two

THE BUTTON NECKLACE

TROON HARRISON

PENGUIN
CANADA

PENGUIN CANADA

Published by the Penguin Group

Penguin Group (Canada), 90 Eglinton Avenue East, Suite 700, Toronto, Ontario, Canada M4P 2Y3
(a division of Pearson Penguin Canada Inc.)

Penguin Group (USA) Inc., 375 Hudson Street, New York, New York 10014, U.S.A.
Penguin Books Ltd, 80 Strand, London WC2R 0RL, England
Penguin Ireland, 25 St Stephen's Green, Dublin 2, Ireland (a division of Penguin Books Ltd)
Penguin Group (Australia), 250 Camberwell Road, Camberwell, Victoria 3124, Australia
(a division of Pearson Australia Group Pty Ltd)
Penguin Books India Pvt Ltd, 11 Community Centre, Panchsheel Park, New Delhi – 110 017, India
Penguin Group (NZ), cnr Airborne and Rosedale Roads, Albany, Auckland 1310, New Zealand
(a division of Pearson New Zealand Ltd)
Penguin Books (South Africa) (Pty) Ltd, 24 Sturdee Avenue, Rosebank, Johannesburg 2196,
South Africa

Penguin Books Ltd, Registered Offices: 80 Strand, London WC2R 0RL, England

First published 2005

1 2 3 4 5 6 7 8 9 10 (WEB)

Design: Matthews Communications Design Inc.

Manufactured in Canada.

LIBRARY AND ARCHIVES CANADA CATALOGUING IN PUBLICATION

Harrison, Troon, 1958–
Millie : the button necklace / Troon Harrison.

(Our Canadian girl)
"Millie : book two".
ISBN 0-14-305025-7

I. Title. II. Title: Button necklace. III. Series.

PS8565.A6587M463 2005 jC813'.54 C2005-900217-4

Visit the Penguin Group (Canada) website at **www.penguin.ca**

In memory of every person who worked for the enfranchisement of women in Canada

Yukon
Northwest Territories
Nunavut
British Columbia
Alberta
Saskatchewan
Manitoba

Marks the location of the story

Millie's Story

In 1914, Canada joined its allies in Europe to fight in World War I. In Toronto, the war affected many things. The Canadian National Exhibition grounds became a shooting range where soldiers practised their aim using wooden targets. The University of Toronto campus became a training camp where soldiers practised drills and where the army pitched tents. A wall of sandbags was built in front of City Hall to remind people of the trenches being dug in France. Army recruiters toured the streets, asking men to sign up. Many Canadian men did go to war, leaving their homes by train and then taking ships across the Atlantic Ocean to England.

One man who joined up is Millie's father, and she misses him very much. Millie has promised her father that she'll stay out of trouble while he's away, but this is becoming a hard promise to keep. When Millie starts a new school, she reunites with Edwina and learns that Edwina's mother is a suffragist. Suffragists were usually well-educated women. Many of them had jobs in a time when most women stayed at home with their families. Suffragists were often journalists, doctors, lawyers, or teachers. They believed that women should be allowed to vote in federal and provincial political elections. They were also interested in social reform. They wanted to pass laws to promote children's health care and education, and laws to provide care for children who were orphaned or abused. As more and more men left to fight the war, many women found themselves living alone for the first time. Factories and other businesses hired female workers to replace the men who had left. This was a time of change for women and their rights. The suffrage movement reached its peak in 1914, with more than ten thousand male and female members. By 1918, all women over twenty-one years of age had gained the federal vote. Some also had gained the provincial vote, but certain provinces were slow to give voting rights to women. Women in Quebec could not vote in provincial elections until 1940!

Another movement for females that began during this period was the Girl Guides. Young girls could join a group called the Rosebuds (now called the Brownies).

There were no other groups like this for girls, where they could do such outdoor activities as camping, learning to tie knots, and cooking over fires. Many mothers were unsure whether these behaviours were suitable for their daughters, who should have been inside at home, learning to embroider and play music instead. Millie longs to join the Rosebud group. How can she convince her mother to let her?

Millie soon finds herself accompanying Edwina and her mother to the poorest and most dangerous area of Toronto: St. John's Ward (often called The Ward). This area was roughly bordered by Yonge Street, College Street, University Avenue, and Queen Street. Many immigrant families lived there in extreme poverty, without running water or toilets, in crowded and dirty slum homes. Millie has been warned to stay away from this part of the city, but instead she makes friends with some poor children there. While learning more about the suffrage movement and trying to help her new friends, Millie moves closer and closer to danger. Her chance to join the Rosebuds, her friendships, and even her safety are all put at risk.

CHAPTER Nº 1

It was a beautiful morning in September 1914, with blue sky over Toronto. The leaves on the trees lining St. George Street were tinged yellow. As we walked, Father hummed "Onward Christian Soldiers," his lips curved in a smile beneath his moustache. I didn't hum with him.

This was the worst morning of my life.

Every step took me closer to my new school and the moment we'd say goodbye. I wished I could hold Father's hand, but I was too old. A lump swelled in my throat.

"Why do you have to go to England?" I asked.

"Everyone says the war will be over by Christmas."

"Aye, true enough," my father responded. "So dinna fret, Millie. We shall not be parted long. But a man must do what he can. His Majesty's Royal Navy will be in need of engineers such as myself."

We reached College Street, which was busy with carriages and automobiles. Soldiers with guns marched past as their drill sergeant bellowed commands. Yesterday, Father and I had seen white tents being raised on the university campus. Soon, companies of soldiers would train there. Soon, they would all be far away in Europe, gone to fight the Germans. Father had taken me to Union Station to watch troop trains chugging out. Soldiers leaned from carriage windows, waving their caps. On the platform, women hid their grief beneath the flutter of handkerchiefs. Their eyes shone as they stared after loved ones.

Father and I crossed to the south side of College Street.

"Ye'll be fine, Millie," my father said. "You'll make new friends in the twinkling of an eye."

I don't want new friends, I longed to protest, but I said nothing. It had not been Father's idea to send me to a different school.

When I had returned from my summer holiday in the Kawartha Lakes, Mother had said, "Millie, I've made arrangements for you to attend Bishop Strachan. You'll be with other girls from good families, learning languages, dancing, and ladylike deportment."

Already, my holidays seemed long ago. Hurrying beside Father, closer to the new school filled with strangers, I wished I could have stayed at the lake with my cousins. I wished I were paddling a canoe or tucking up my dress to wade among water lilies. Nobody at the lake cared about dancing lessons. I didn't want to learn languages. I just wanted Father to stay home, and I wanted to climb trees with Tommy, the boy next door, and play my mouth organ. I wanted Toronto to return to the way it had been, before the streets were filled with soldiers, recruiters, and news of war. Why did everything have to change?

"Here we are then, and a grand place it is," Father interrupted my thoughts. We stood outside Bishop Strachan School: an old brick house with several wings, three storeys, and a belvedere on the roof. I stared at the pillars and balconies while chattering girls in uniform jostled up the front steps.

My stomach cramped. "Don't go, Father, please," I begged.

He hugged me; the chain of his pocket watch pressed into my cheek. "Whist, lass," he soothed. "Your mother will need your help while I'm away. It's time to grow up, Millie. Do ye ken? Ye'll need to be cheerful—and dinna cause trouble."

I nodded silently while Father patted my back. "Off with ye then," he said, "and meet the other young ladies. I'll bring ye a Christmas present when I come home."

I nodded, biting my lip, trying not to cry while I smiled at Father. His blue eyes twinkled and he ran his hand over his curly black hair, stiff with pomade. Then he was off, striding down College

"Don't go, Father, please," I begged. He hugged me; the chain of his pocket watch pressed into my cheek.

Street, humming again. I watched until he shrank to a little stick man. He was gone. I was scared that I would never see him again.

My face stiff, I crossed the lawn beneath the trees and went up the steps. I did not look at the other girls, and when I heard laughter behind me, I didn't turn. Perhaps they were laughing at me. Inside, a teacher shepherded us to the chapel. We sang hymns and then prayed for the soldiers going overseas to fight for King George V of England, who was our king, too. I imagined that right now my father might be kissing my mother goodbye, tickling my baby sister's cheeks, and heading to the station.

Afterward, we were sent to our classrooms. In mine, a blond girl was cleaning the blackboard. I found myself a desk by the windows, where I could stare at the blue sky. Around me, other girls joked and thumped down books. No one spoke to me. I stared at the top of my desk where someone had scratched her initials. Suddenly, something hard and white bounced off my arm. I jumped and turned around. A piece of chalk lay on the floor behind my seat. Who had thrown it? I looked up slowly, my cheeks burning.

The girl at the board had turned to face the class and was holding another piece of chalk. Her midi blouse was a size too large and she had pinned a spray of yellow chrysanthemums onto the front. Her mischievous eyes laughed at me. "Millie MacCallum!" she said. "What are *you* doing here?"

I gasped in amazement, and then I laughed too. Edwina and I had met at the lakes on our summer holidays and had tried to balance together on a log boom. Edwina was the most fun of any girl I knew; she was as much fun as Tommy.

"Edwina! Are you here at—"

"Miss Sinclair, if you have finished cleaning the board, you may be seated."

Miss Haversham, our teacher, entered, wearing a long skirt and plain white blouse fastened with a cameo brooch.

Edwina set the cloth down and moved toward her desk.

"And, Miss Sinclair," said the teacher, "kindly remove that flower. A school uniform is not a suitable garment for decoration."

Edwina, standing near me in the aisle, stiffened her back. I saw the creases straighten in her blouse.

"This flower is not decoration," she replied in a serious tone. "Yellow is the colour of the suffragist movement."

There was absolute silence as girls stared in disbelief. Edwina was talking back to a teacher! My heart beat loudly.

"And what is it about the suffragist movement that you wish to draw our attention to?" Miss Haversham asked.

"My mother says that women should have the vote," Edwina replied clearly. "She says that she pays taxes but she can't vote for who spends her money. She says that taxes without represent … representation is tyranny. If women could vote, there would be better laws for children's health and education."

The teacher's look became stern. "You are very bold," she said. "My classroom is neither a political rally nor a suffragist meeting. You will remove those flowers, sit down, and open your mathematics text to page three."

For one breathless moment, neither Edwina nor the teacher moved. *Please don't argue,* I begged Edwina in my thoughts. If Edwina landed in trouble during the very first hour of school, how could I be her friend? I had just promised Father that I'd not cause trouble while he was away. Then, slowly, Edwina unpinned the flowers, and the teacher moved to the board. Edwina walked up the aisle to sit two desks behind me. A sigh gusted from the girls as they breathed again.

All through mathematics, I thought about Edwina. I remembered how she let the wind blow her hat overboard on the steamboat because she hated hats. She hadn't said anything in the summer about suffragists. My own mother seldom said anything about them either. Sometimes the *Globe* newspaper printed editorials about women's rights and petitions to pass new laws for women. Once, my father had said that if women ruled the country the way they ruled their homes, the world would be a better place. But my mother had said that a woman's place was in the home and she didn't need to work outside it.

Suddenly, a tiny ball of paper landed on my exercise book. I made sure that Miss Haversham was writing sums on the board before unfolding it. *Wednesday, tea at my house? E!* I read the penciled words. When I glanced back, Edwina grinned. The chrysanthemums lay on her exercise book, bright yellow on the page.

"Miss MacCallum, eyes forward!" Miss Haversham snapped, and I swivelled to my sums. I hoped that Edwina would not land us both in trouble before Wednesday.

CHAPTER No. 2

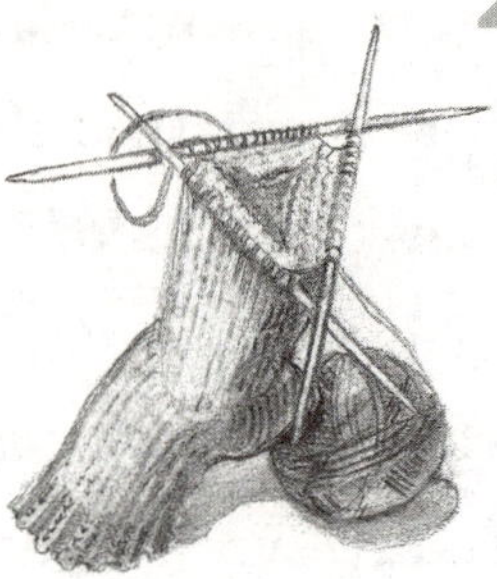

After classes ended for the day, Edwina and I sat on the front lawn. I was waiting for Flo, our maid, to walk me home because I wasn't allowed to walk alone in the city. I wished I were waiting for Father. I imagined him rattling east on a train, surrounded by soldiers, becoming farther away every minute.

"Hey," said Edwina, "do you want to start Rosebuds with me?"

"What?"

"Rosebuds—they're like Girl Guides, only younger. We'd learn things like tying knots and cooking over fires. Last spring, the Rosebuds and the Guides camped in a ravine and all the mothers came every night to check that they were all right. No flaming tents or savage beasts!"

Edwina rolled her eyes dramatically, and I laughed and forgot about troop trains.

"The school has a Guides group; we could start Rosebuds!"

"I'll ask my mother," I promised. Tommy would be impressed if I learned how to tie complicated knots. Maybe then he'd let me join the Boys Only club in his tree house. Or maybe I wouldn't want to; the longer Edwina talked about the Rosebuds, the more it sounded like an exciting Girls Only club. Life in the city would be much more fun now that Edwina was my friend.

After Flo arrived, Edwina and I trailed her home. Trees cast long shadows on the rows of big brick houses on St. George Street.

"Where do you live?" I asked Edwina.

"At Huron and Bloor," she said. "I'm allowed to walk by myself. Mother's too busy to come with me."

"Why?"

"She's a journalist. She works all hours."

"She works?" I gaped at Edwina. I didn't know any mothers who had jobs. All the ones I knew stayed home and made sure that suppers were hot on the tables when the fathers came home.

"She writes for the *World* newspaper," Edwina said. "What does your mother do?"

"She takes care of Louisa May, my baby sister, and goes to Charity Society meetings and … um, has friends over for tea. She embroiders—"

"Come along, Miss Millie. I haven't got all day!" cried Flo from the front steps of our house.

I rolled my eyes at Edwina. Our gardener, Bill, who was trimming the grass along the pavement, gave a sympathetic laugh.

"Afternoon, Miss Millie and Miss Edwina," he said, touching his cap.

"You two know each other?" I asked.

Edwina nodded. "Bill used to garden for us, too, before my father …"

"Before what?" I asked, but Edwina just shrugged and stared at the ground, and Bill shook his head at me. I was mystified, but before I could ask any more questions, Flo called again from the door.

"Goodbye," I said to Edwina.

"Ask about Rosebuds and tea!" she reminded me and then continued chatting with Bill as I went up the path under the maples.

In our front hall, I stroked my fingers over the smooth marble statue of St. Francis. It had been brought from England, from the house where my mother grew up with fifteen servants and a stable of racehorses. I wondered if my father would visit there or if he'd be too busy building navy ships. In the kitchen Bertha, our cook and housekeeper, gave me an apple turnover and a glass of milk. Then I followed the sound of Louisa May's crying and found Mother rocking her in the nursery. Mother's eyes were pink as if she had been crying, too, but that couldn't have been right because she never cried.

I waited until Louisa May fell asleep, her chubby fists clutching a teething biscuit.

"Tell me about your first day of school," my mother said, sitting in her rocker and picking up knitting needles and a ball of grey yarn.

I sat on the rug and watched her loop stitches over the needles. "What are you making?"

"Socks for soldiers," she replied. "Though, gracious knows, this wool is coarse enough to give a man blisters."

As she knitted, I told her about Edwina and being invited for tea and the Rosebuds. "Can I join?" I asked.

"I don't know," my mother said, sounding tired. "What do they wear?"

"They have a uniform that the mothers make," I said. "A midi and a skirt and a scarf. Could you make me one?"

"I don't know," my mother said again, which was strange because she hardly ever said that. She tucked a strand of hair back into her chignon. "I think you would be better at home, Millie, learning how to heel socks. And I have bandages for France that need rolling."

"Socks!" I cried in dismay. "Bandages?"

Mother frowned. "Just because we don't go to war like the men doesn't mean that we can be idle. Bandages and socks are as necessary in the war as anything else. And these Rosebuds sound like tomboys. Your father and I are sending you to Bishop Strachan to learn ladylike behaviour."

"But, Mother!" I cried. "It's not fair—"

"Please do not argue," she interrupted sternly. "Today, your father went away. Flo is leaving us to work in a factory for higher wages. With the men going to war, the factories are hiring women. This afternoon, Bill gave his notice and enlisted to fight. I have enough problems, Millicent, without a fuss from you. This war will ask sacrifices of us all."

I stared at the intricate pattern on the Turkish rug and felt hot with rebellion. *I didn't ask for there to be a war,* I thought. Why did a war in some far-off place mean that I couldn't be a Rosebud and learn to tie knots? Tommy would never let me join his club, and I wasn't even allowed to join one of my own.

Then I thought about what my mother had said. Without Flo, who would light the fires and clean the house? Who would walk me to school? Without Bill, who would weed the flower beds and drive my mother around in our Model T?

I glanced at Mother's face. She looked pale and sad. Maybe she was thinking about Father, rushing east on a troop train. Remembering my promise to him, I felt guilty. It was selfish to ask Mother to sew a uniform when she had so many other problems. I swallowed down my disappointment in little chunks, piece by piece. *Maybe another time,* I tried to console myself. *Maybe another time Mother will agree to my plea to join the Rosebuds*. Finally, Mother looked up and gave me a kind smile.

"Ask your new friend if her mother will send me a note. Then you can go for tea."

"Thank you," I said and tried to make my lips curve right up when I smiled back.

CHAPTER No. 3

On Tuesday, Edwina brought the note from her mother. After school, I waited breathlessly while Mother slit the envelope with her ivory-handled knife.

"What does it say?" I asked. "May I go?"

Mother read the note, then smiled. "I'm happy you're making a new friend, Millie. I have heard of this family. Mr. Sinclair died tragically two years ago of apoplexy. He was a respected barrister. Now I hear that poor Mrs. Sinclair works at the *World* to support her family. What an unsuitable life for a woman." My mother sighed in sympathy.

"May I go?"

"Today is Flo's last day. I will have to walk you to school from now on, Millie. Tomorrow I have a meeting to attend and I can't walk you to Edwina's for tea."

"Mother," I said desperately, "Edwina and I can walk to and from school together. That way we won't be alone. I'm old enough now—"

At that moment, we were interrupted by Bertha. "Begging your pardon, Ma'am," she said, "but Bill's in the kitchen asking for his last wages."

Upstairs in the nursery, Louisa May began crying. Mother rose to her feet.

"Tell Bill I shall bring his wages shortly," she said.

"Mother, please," I beseeched.

She gave me a worried frown and then, as Louisa May's crying continued, she nodded. "This war is turning the world topsy-turvy," she complained. "You may walk with Edwina, I suppose. But for goodness' sake, stay together and do not speak to anyone."

The next morning, I met Edwina outside my house. Her hair was braided in plaits and tied with yellow ribbons. "What do you think?" She waved a pigtail at me.

"Miss Haversham will know."

"There's no rule that says what colour ribbons you must wear." Edwina grinned mischievously. "And look, I brought you some, too."

She reached into her satchel and pulled out two more bright yellow ribbons.

"Edwina, I don't—"

"You're not scared of Miss Haversham, are you?"

"N-no," I said doubtfully. "It's just ... about the suffragists. I don't know if I support their cause."

Edwina stopped walking and fixed me with a serious stare. "Do you think men are smarter than women?"

"No, of course not."

"Then women should have an equal say in what goes on. Do you want to grow up and let your husband decide everything?"

"No," I replied. "But my mother says that a woman's place is in the home and she doesn't need to worry about anything else."

"Not all women," argued Edwina.

My mind raced. Now that my father and other men had gone away to war, many women would be left alone. Maybe they *would* need to worry about things outside their own houses. My Aunt Mary, in the Kawartha Lakes, had shown me the skills that Native women had. She was strong enough to paddle a big canoe alone and smart enough to build one. I didn't think she would need my Uncle Eddy to make decisions for her. Then I thought about Aunt Mary's friend Mrs. O'Neill, who lived in a cabin on a hill. After Mrs. O'Neill's husband had died, she had raised her children alone, shot a moose, and planted many gardens. In winter, she crossed the drifts on snowshoes. She seemed to live outside her home as much as inside it.

"Suit yourself," Edwina said, pushing the ribbons back into her satchel. She strode on with her nose in the air. Maybe now she wouldn't want to be my friend. Maybe she was right about the suffragists.... I didn't want to grow up and have some boy, like Tommy, boss me around.

"Wait! I'll wear them!" I said.

At school, Edwina and I sat at our usual desks for first class. When Miss Haversham walked in, my heart beat loudly, but she only asked us to open our books. It wasn't until after class that she called our names and kept us behind.

"Yellow ribbons," she said dryly. "Might they have a meaning beyond mere adornment?"

My cheeks flushed, but Edwina's voice was steady when she replied, "Women are as smart as men."

"Indeed, but their roles might not be the same, Edwina. Different skills are needed for different roles in life."

"My mother works and pays taxes. You work, too. Why can't you vote?"

I stared at my boot toes. I couldn't believe Edwina would talk this way to a teacher.

Miss Haversham's gaze did not flicker. "What

impertinence, Edwina! You are like a terrier about this topic. Why?"

"My father supported the cause. He told me before he—when he took ill … he made me promise to support my mother!"

Edwina's eyes shone but no tears spilled out. My chest felt tight with a mixture of emotions. If anything tragic happened to my father in the war—! I couldn't bear the thought of it. I would promise him anything. But, I reminded myself, when he left, I *had* promised something: not to cause trouble. I had a guilty feeling that I was not keeping my promise. Miss Haversham turned her gaze to me.

"Why are you wearing yellow, Millicent?"

I was tongue-tied. "I—I'm Edwina's friend," I stuttered. "And I don't think girls should have to stay indoors when boys can climb trees."

There was a long silence during which I heard Edwina sniff back tears. Miss Haversham looked thoughtful, then her lips twitched as though she were trying not to smile.

My cheeks flushed, but Edwina's voice was steady when she replied, "Women are as smart as men."

"Take the ribbons off, girls," she said. "You are entitled to your opinions, but you will not flaunt them in my classroom. Any more of this and I shall send each of your mothers a note. I will not warn you again."

We untied the ribbons and were sent out to play croquet on the lawn. Waiting for my turn, I imagined Mother's face if Miss Haversham wrote her a note. Mother would not let me be Edwina's friend then—and she certainly would not change her mind about letting me join the Rosebuds. I had to steer clear of any more trouble.

CHAPTER No 4

After school, Edwina and I hurried to her house. It was smaller than mine and fronted a busier street. Edwina led us up the wide stone steps to the front door. Inside, the hallway was cluttered with piles of newspapers. Tennis rackets leaned against the wall. The rug was faded, and a bowl containing bread crusts sat on one edge.

"Do you have a dog?" I asked.

"No, that's just for strays. We let them in sometimes."

Strays! Bertha would never let a stray dog into our house. Strays were dirty or had fleas.

"We're home!" Edwina shouted and led me into a small room that held a desk heaped with books. Mrs. Sinclair turned from her typewriter. Her eyes were very bright. She seemed older and sharper somehow than my mother was. Everything about her ended in a point: her elbows, her wrist bones, her nose. Even her smile had pointy corners.

"Why, girls, you're just in time. I'm going out to do some research. You must come."

"I'm hungry," Edwina said.

"Get yourself a bite then." Mrs. Sinclair turned back to her typewriter. I watched, fascinated, as her fingers flew over the round white keys and the metal arms leapt up and hit the paper, making crisp letters.

"Fold some more brochures while you eat!" Mrs. Sinclair called as we went to the kitchen. Edwina took the lid off a tin and cut us huge slices of fruitcake. Bertha would never have given me so much; she would've scolded about the price of currants and ruining my supper.

"Did your cook make this?" I asked.

"My sister Ivy. Both my sisters study at the university."

Edwina cleared a place at the table, pushing aside dirty cups with gold rims and a stack of paper. While she ate her cake, she took pieces of paper and folded them into three, so that each piece became a brochure. To make each one lie flat, she ran a rolling pin over the edges.

"What are they?"

"Suffragist brochures. The women hand them out on the streets."

I picked one up. "Social Reform" stated the large letters across the top. Then, in small print below, were more words: "Although it is widely agreed that women are the arbiters of family moral values, it is less widely accepted that the voices of women would make a difference in the state of our country. Yet one belief must, by the laws of logic, lead to the second. For if women are the caretakers of their children's moral learning, health, education, and fitness for life, must it not follow that women are ideally suited to such roles in the broader realm of politics? If women were to be given the right to vote, their care would extend to the citizens of our nation to the benefit of all. Female voters would lend their experienced voices to those proposing legislation for social reform, including temperance and bills responsible for the welfare, health, and education of children."

I put the brochure down, puzzling over its long words.

"It means that women can make laws, too," Edwina said. "My mother says we need more laws about child welfare."

I nodded and began to help fold brochures. There seemed to be hundreds of pieces of paper.

"Come along, girls," Mrs. Sinclair called.

I wrapped the rest of my cake in my hankie and put it in my pocket. Then we followed Mrs. Sinclair out the front door and south into the city. Mrs. Sinclair was not a tall woman but she moved fast, her short skirt flapping at her ankles. She did not wear a hat and her hair fluttered messily. My mother never set out without a hat; she had round boxes full of them. They had sweeping brims trimmed with ribbons and silk flowers. Had Edwina's mother forgotten her own hat in her hurry?

"Where are we going?" Edwina panted as we headed east along College Street.

"To view conditions among the poor in The Ward," Mrs. Sinclair replied briskly. "I have an article to write about the appalling lack of amenities in the homes there. It's high time that the city provided immigrant families with better houses."

The Ward, I thought in horror. We were heading into The Ward? The Ward was the poorest part of Toronto; Mother spoke in hushed tones about its taverns and vices. Father had told me that I must never go there, that it was filled with disease, crime, filth, and unemployed foreigners.

I felt worse the closer we came to Yonge Street. My mother thought that I was safely at Edwina's house, and instead I was disobeying everything I'd been told.

"Mrs. Sinclair—" I gasped, and she turned to let Edwina and me catch up.

"Now, girls. Stay close and you'll be fine," she said, as if reading my thoughts. She charged on and I had missed my chance to tell her that I wanted to go home instead. Edwina winked and skipped after her mother. Terrified of being separated from them, I followed miserably, filled with dread. The streets grew crowded with streetcars and carriages. Horses neighed and churned up dust with their hooves. From tavern doorways wafted the stench of smoke and stale beer, and the babble of different languages. I hunched my shoulders, making myself as small as possible, and scuttled past, my gaze fixed on the ground. A man pushed a wooden cart filled with strawberry and chocolate ice cream. When a skinny dog ran past, stopped, and peed on the wheels, the man shouted *"Basta!"*

Edwina giggled. "He must think it speaks Italian!"

Ragged boys jostled past, chasing a hoop. On a street corner, a man with a scraggly black beard sat on a bucket and played an accordion. Small children who had filthy legs and scabs on their faces danced in front of him. Other children called out in a language I didn't know and stared with dark eyes as we passed. A woman—with rings through her ears!—sat on a dirty step and drank from a bottle, smacking her lips. I rushed past, terrified she might speak to me.

Mrs. Sinclair plunged down a narrow side street. Shabby houses leaned at angles, their yards filled with rusty metal, empty crates, and sacks of rubbish. Beneath a pile of refuse, I spotted a sleek body and bright eyes. I choked back a yell and grabbed Edwina's arm.

"There's a rat!" I pointed but it had disappeared deeper into the pile. My nose filled with the stench of urine and sickly rotting things. I felt as if I were suffocating. My forehead and back were damp with sweat. There were no trees here, no green lawns, and not even a sidewalk. We hurried along the road's edge, our ankles twisting as we crossed ruts. Danger seemed to press in from every side.

"Here we are," Mrs. Sinclair announced and rapped at the door of a—shed? Surely it was not a house. Was it where a man worked or where tools were stored? It had only one crooked window, covered with grime. The door opened with a squeal of worn hinges that made me jump. I stared fearfully into the darkness.

A scrawny woman in a faded dress stared back. A pale, whimpering child clung to her legs. The woman nodded at Edwina's mother without a smile. "You've come then. Best git this done sharpish; I've to leave fer work."

Mrs. Sinclair stepped inside and Edwina and I jostled behind. Even Edwina was quiet now. When my eyes adjusted to the dimness, I saw wooden walls, without paper or paint. They were smeared with dirt. Three stools surrounded a battered table, and a woodstove with a rusty top stood crookedly in a corner. This was a house? People lived here? I could hardly believe my eyes!

Mrs. Sinclair whipped a notebook out of her leather satchel. She glanced around and began scribbling notes.

"Running water?" she asked.

"Git it from the pump down the street."

"Where do you all sleep?"

The woman gestured to another room. It held one sagging bed frame with a stained mattress and tattered blankets heaped on the board floor. Then, I saw the most incredible thing of all: on one of those heaps, a baby slept. It was naked but for a diaper. A rash spread across its chest, and flies buzzed around its face.

"How many children did you say?"

"Four. Me oldest is about ten. Then there's Bertie, an' Ellie here, an' the baby."

"Any more rooms?" Mrs. Sinclair asked, still scribbling in her notebook.

The woman lifted the whimpering child and crossed the kitchen to shove open another door. Edwina and I ducked under the low frame. I wanted to stay as close to Mrs. Sinclair as I could.

We were in an addition with a sloping roof. Withered carrots and wrinkled potatoes lay in a crate beside a pile of rotting scrap lumber. A stinking dark hole in one corner was surrounded by crooked boards; it was the toilet. I pressed my arm across my face. I thought I'd choke.

"Let's go out," Edwina whispered. We went to the street and perched on the splintered front steps of the house.

"This is horrible," Edwina said, and I nodded. I could hardly endure being here; my heart fluttered in panic. I wanted to run and run, back to St. George Street with its gracious brick houses full of potted plants, framed paintings, wallpaper, pianos, and shining floors.

"Hey," said Edwina suddenly, "here come some children."

The girl looked about our age. Her bare toes had ragged nails and her dress only reached her knees. Her long hair was the same colour as mine, but it wasn't curled in ringlets. Instead, it hung straight, dull with dust. Beside her ambled a boy of about eight, with freckles on his face below his flat cap. They stopped and the girl folded her skinny arms across her chest.

"Wotcher doin' 'ere?" she asked crossly.

"My mother's inside talking to your mother," Edwina explained.

The boy wiped his nose on his sleeve, then wiggled his tongue at us through the gap in his front teeth.

"Wot she doin' that fer?" the girl asked, her eyes narrowed in her thin face.

"She's writing about the bad houses for the *World* paper. She thinks the city should knock them down and build something better for you to live in."

The girl pondered this, drawing circles in the dust with her toes. "Wot then—you rich toffs or somefink?" she said scornfully. "You ain't got nothing better to do than poke yer noses in other blighters' 'ouses?"

Edwina flushed. "We're trying to help. Do you like living here?"

The girl shrugged. "Got to live someplace, 'aven't we?"

I felt awful. It would be horrible if strangers came to my house and asked my mother questions and felt sorry for us. I thought of that baby lying with the flies while my little sister, Louisa May, lay at home in a shining cradle, under lace-edged coverlets.

"I'm Millie and this is Edwina," I told the girl. "What's your name?"

"Name's Molly an' this 'ere's me brovver, Bertie. Quit pokin out yer tongue!" She cuffed Bertie's ears. He poked his tongue out at her instead and laughed gleefully.

Suddenly I remembered my cake. I pulled it out and handed it to Molly, still wrapped in my hankie.

"Wot's this?" she asked suspiciously.

"Fruitcake."

Molly shovelled some into her mouth and chewed, then smiled for the first time. Her smile lit up her face, making her look different. "Cor blimey, that's the real goods," she said. "'Ere,

Bertie, you 'ave the rest. Eat stuff like this every day, do yer?"

Edwina and I nodded.

"Lumme," said Molly in tones of wonder. "All them currants an' it ain't even Christmas. Me pot and pan loved currants. 'Course, we ain't likely to see 'im again. Me maw says 'e's done a bunk."

"What?" I asked, watching Bertie lick my handkerchief. I hoped he didn't have any horrible diseases.

"Me father's scarpered," Molly said impatiently. "'E said 'e were off to find work, but 'e's niver come back fer two months. Good riddance, Maw says. 'E were always in the Sow and Whistle drinkin' away all the money. A dry gullet were 'is problem. Now me maw's cleanin' 'otel rooms on Yonge Street an' says we're 'eadin for life on the streets."

"Who looks after the baby?" Edwina asked.

"Me, o' course," snorted Molly. "That's the last of us, Maw says. Poor little teapot lid."

"How come you talk so funny?" Edwina asked.

Molly scowled. "Nofink wrong wiv me talk. It's 'ow everyone talks back 'ome in London—"

"Got any apples in yer pockets?" interrupted Bertie with a look of longing.

I shook my head.

"Cor," he said sadly. "Me gob just waters thinkin' 'bout apples."

Edwina and I had the same idea at the same moment.

"The orchard near school—" I said.

"Yes, we'll use pillowcases. Tomorrow at dusk?"

"Yes."

"You know where a bloke can crib apples?" Bertie asked, and I nodded.

"We'll bring you some tomorrow," I said, giving a confident smile.

Mrs. Sinclair had finished talking to Bertie and Molly's mother, and she joined us outside. She smiled at the children and turned to Edwina and me.

"Off we go, girls," she said, tucking her satchel beneath one arm.

"You can keep my hankie," I told Bertie, and he stuffed it into a pocket as Edwina and I waved goodbye.

Following Mrs. Sinclair home, I blocked out the stern voice in my head telling me that I must be crazy. This idea about stealing apples was the most foolish notion I'd had yet in my life.

CHAPTER No. 5

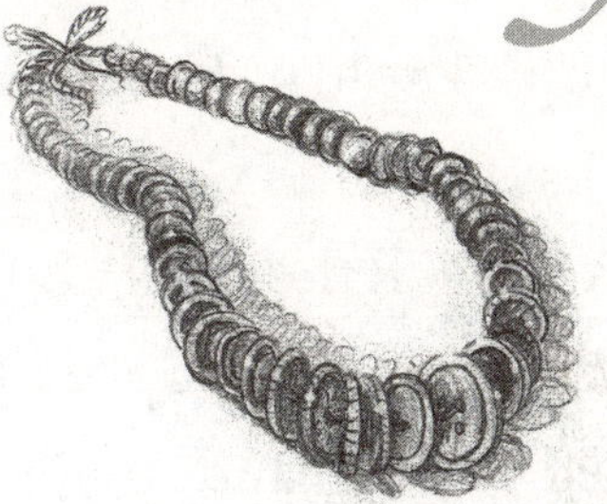

"How did you get out?" Edwina asked the next evening when we met in the shadows beneath the trees.

"Bertha's gone to her room, and Mother's writing Father a letter," I whispered. "Hurry, before they notice!"

We ran down St. George Street, tree trunks and lights in windows blurring past. I had never been out alone at night. Everything seemed mysterious and larger, as though darkness made things grow. We panted along College Street until we reached the orchard's stone wall. Several buildings away stood our school; I searched for the familiar outline of its belvedere. When I saw it so close by, I imagined the boarders preparing for bed and felt comforted.

"Boost me up," I told Edwina. I stepped into her cupped hands and wrapped my fingers around the stones of the wall. Edwina shoved and soon I was sitting on top of the orchard's wall. I reached down and gripped Edwina's hands. Her boots scrabbled on the rough stones, dislodging pebbles. Suddenly, she heaved into me and we overbalanced and crashed onto the orchard grass. We lay still, waiting for a dog to bark and stifling nervous laughter with our hands.

"Come on," Edwina hissed.

Under the trees, a few rotting apples squelched under our boots, but many still clung to the branches. I jumped, grabbing at the round, ripe fruit. A twig scratched my face and I clamped my mouth shut over a yell. Edwina held open the pillowcase she'd hidden inside her blouse, and I placed the apples in it. Their sweet ripe smell flavoured the cool air, and their skins were smooth.

"We'd better go," I whispered nervously.

"Just two more."

I jumped again. When I landed, a twig snapped and we held still, listening. It was almost dark now. I tried not to think about what we had to do next, because it made my skin crawl with fear.

"Let's go," I pleaded.

It was harder getting over the wall with the apples, and when we finally made it to the top, we were panting. I grabbed the pillowcase of apples and swung my legs over to slide down.

"Hush," hissed Edwina, and I heard footsteps coming along the pavement. Edwina gripped my arm too late; I was already sliding down the wall with the pillowcase banging my back. I landed with a thump. As I jumped up, Edwina landed beside me—and a large dark shape came toward us. The streetlights had come on while we were in the orchard, and we were beneath one.

"Oi, stop right there!" a man cried, but Edwina and I began to run east along College Street.

I couldn't hear whether anyone was chasing us, but I felt the dark shape just behind me. At any moment, fingers would dig into my shoulders and a voice would cry, "Stop! Thief!" The skin on the back of my neck prickled. I gulped great mouthfuls of air and ran until my lungs burned. Finally, Edwina and I staggered to a walk and I glanced back. No one followed. We walked on, shoulder to shoulder.

"We're nearly there," Edwina said. The streets were busier and the buildings dirtier. Rough laughter floated from an alley, and two men staggered from a tavern. Edwina and I hung back, waiting until they reached the corner of Yonge Street.

"There's Bertie," Edwina said. He stood in the doorway of a closed shop, glancing around to check the street.

"Fancy a bit of fun, girl? I can show it to you!" hollered one of the drunks, and I saw Molly press

As I jumped up, Edwina landed beside me—and a large dark shape came toward us.

against the shop door. Bertie jumped in front with his fists up. "Yer wouldn't know fun if yer saw it, Mister!" he shouted.

The men laughed and went on. Edwina and I fell into the doorway, speechless from running and fear.

"Yes!" shouted Bertie. "A whole hopping pot of apples! See, Moll, I told yer they'd come."

He plunged his arm into the pillowcase and pulled out a smooth, crisp apple. He crunched it happily as juice ran down his grubby chin. Molly smiled at us as she reached for an apple.

"Ta," she said. "Yer real china plate. I didn't fink you'd come."

"Did your father come back?" Edwina asked.

Bertie rolled his eyes and spat out apple seeds. "'E's probably in the rusty nail by now!"

"Where?"

"Jail," Molly said. She bit into her apple.

Edwina and I were silent with horror while Molly and Bertie crunched loudly. It was awful when my father went to war, but to have a drunk father in prison was far worse! I couldn't imagine what the inside of a jail was like; maybe something like Molly's house, with smelly air and dirty walls—a place you couldn't escape from, even though people lived nearby in mansions.

I wished that I could take Molly home, that Bertha could bake turnovers for her, and that my mother could wash and curl Molly's hair with her gentle fingers.

"Wotcher starin' at?" Molly asked.

"Nothing—I mean, we should go home," I stammered.

"Fill yer Davy Crocketts," Molly told Bertie, and they stuffed as many apples into their pockets as they could. Molly rolled up the rest of them in her apron.

"Oi, I nearly fergot this," Molly said, reaching to her throat. She pulled a necklace off and handed it to me. It was made from buttons of different colours and sizes threaded onto red yarn. "Fer you," she said shyly. "'Cause I ain't got no other friends."

"Thank you!" I said in surprise, slipping the warm buttons over my head.

"See ya lata, hot potata," Bertie called and he skipped south toward the slum, while Molly rushed to catch up.

Edwina and I turned the other way. We linked arms; I could feel that Edwina was holding herself stiff, too. We kept our eyes down, walked fastest under the streetlights, and held our breath all the way to St. George Street. Beneath the trees, we hugged goodbye and Edwina ran on alone while I sneaked around to the back and climbed our fence. I scrambled up the silver maple and shinnied along a limb, wishing Tommy could see me. He was probably asleep already. He didn't know the half of what I could do. I was as good as any boy in his stupid club—and so was Edwina, and Molly, too.

I climbed over the windowsill into my room and slipped off my dress. It was torn and stained from my climb over the wall. Bertha would scold me, but as long as she didn't show Mother, I'd be all right. Although, since Father had left, Mother didn't seem as interested as usual in domestic crises. So, maybe I'd get away with my escapade, since I hadn't been run over or abducted by a drunk—or whatever it was that happened to girls in the city's darkness. I shivered and slipped into my cozy bed, with Molly's gift under my pillow.

The next day, Edwina and I walked to school as usual. "You get caught?" she asked, and I shook my head.

"You?"

"No," said Edwina. "My mother was at a temperance meeting. My sisters were at a dance to raise funds for the war effort."

"Lucky for us," I said, but I spoke too soon.

When we reached school, we were sent straight to Miss Popham's office. Our principal sat behind her heavy walnut desk, resting her plump arms on its shiny surface. She fixed us with a stern glare over the spectacles balanced on the end of her nose.

"It has come to my attention," she began in her deep voice, "that certain activities took place last night around 6 P.M. Mr. Nolan, who takes care of our school grounds, was out for a walk when two girls came over the wall of the orchard not far from here."

My shoulder twitched against Edwina's.

"This is *most* disappointing," Miss Popham said. "I am flabbergasted that two girls from this school would engage in such behaviour. I would expect it of hooligans."

"We were picking them for—" I began.

"Do not interrupt," Miss Popham thundered. "You will miss recess for the next week. In your exercise books, you will write one hundred lines: 'I will henceforth behave in a ladylike manner.'"

"Please, Miss, the reason—" I tried again.

"Miss MacCallum," continued Miss Popham, "I am going to write a letter to your mother and recommend that you no longer spend time with Edwina. I think this friendship is a negative influence on you both."

I opened my mouth but before I could protest, Miss Popham opened the door.

"What Millie's trying to say—" began Edwina.

Miss Popham put her hand on Edwina's back and pushed her gently into the hallway. "One hundred lines," she said and closed her door.

We stared at each other miserably.

"Blast!" I muttered, then hoped Miss Popham hadn't heard me curse or I'd get another hundred lines.

At the end of the afternoon, Miss Popham gave us envelopes with our mothers' names on them. When I arrived home, Mother was at the piano playing the "Blue Danube Waltz." She gave me a sideways smile before looking back at her music. I waited while she played; the tune, so sprightly and magical, made my heart feel even heavier.

At last, Mother read the letter, her lips tightening.

"I can scarcely credit that you would do this," she said. "The danger of it! The deceitfulness! What were you thinking?"

"Mo—" I started, but she raised her hand for silence.

"You will not be allowed to visit Edwina or to walk to school with her. I shall take you myself. Miss Popham writes that you and Edwina will be closely supervised at school and will not spend time together there. Go to your room, and stay until sent for. Think how disappointed your father would be if he knew."

I lay on my white coverlet and burned with crossness, even though a breeze wafted through the net curtains. Would my mother write and tell my father? In some faraway place, would he feel angry and be disappointed in me? Would he remember that I'd promised not to cause trouble and know that I'd broken my promise?

Was Edwina banished to her room, too? Our new friendship was over almost before it had begun. In The Ward, Molly and Bertie were still hungry; I would never find out what happened to them. Someone should have helped them properly. Taking them apples was a hare-brained idea; it didn't change anything. I wished Molly could be my friend. I knew the button necklace was the only thing she had to give away.

Mother would never let me join the Rosebuds now. I'd never learn to tie knots and cook over a fire; Tommy would never let me join his club.

Tears leaked from my eyes.

CHAPTER N° 6

In October, frost sparkled when Mother and I walked to school. Sometimes I saw Edwina walking ahead, but I was not allowed to catch up to her. At school, we were in separate classes now. I heard that a teacher had started a Rosebuds group and Edwina had joined. Thinking about this made me miserable. Nowhere else could girls learn to pitch tents and build fires. *I'll have to be an indoor girl all my life,* I thought gloomily. I hated being indoors. It wasn't fair.

One morning, as my class played Bat and Ball on the lawn, I heard a voice call my name. I wandered away from the other girls and stared around. Then, from behind a shed where Mr. Nolan kept flowerpots, I saw Bertie's and Molly's faces peering out. I sidled behind the shed.

"What are you doing here?" I whispered.

"Climbed over the wall fer a lark. See wot the nobs is up to." Bertie grinned mischievously.

Molly gave me a shy smile. "Still got them buttons?"

"Yes, they're in a special place in my room."

"Wish I could see yer 'ouse. 'Spect it's grand," she said wistfully.

I nodded, embarrassed to reply. Molly would be speechless if she saw our bright rugs and drapes, our pantry and icebox filled with food, and the many dresses in my wardrobe.

"Got any grub on yer?" Bertie asked, but I shook my head. "Cold enough to freeze 'ell over," he continued. "I ain't got no ones and twos, see?"

He shook a bare foot at me.

"No shoes?"

"No coats neither," Molly said. Goosebumps ran over her skinny bare arms.

In the distance, the bell rang. "I have to go," I whispered. "I'll bring you something; I'll leave it here after school."

"Ta," Molly said. "Yer a friend in need."

I flitted out and chased after my classmates. At lunch, I hid bread and cheese in my pocket, and after school, I left it behind the shed, wrapped in my hankie, under a broken flowerpot. Mother, waiting at the front, wondered why I was late, but I didn't tell her. After a few days, I took pumpkin tartlets and sliced ham from our pantry and left them under the pot. A crooked *M* was scratched in the soft dirt nearby; perhaps it was the only part of her name that Molly could write. The third time, Molly was waiting for me. She ate my currant bun and we played a game of tiddlywinks I'd brought in my pocket. We pressed our hands over our mouths to stifle our laughter. At home, Bertha complained that she couldn't find half my handkerchiefs. The fourth time, I left empty ammunition rounds from the soldiers' target practice that Tommy had given me. I thought Bertie would like them. For Molly, I left an old sweater that Mother was throwing out and some bread and cheese again. As I came around the shed, Mr. Nolan crossed the grass, glaring fiercely. "What are you doing back here?"

"Looking for something I dropped."

"Huh," he grunted, as if he didn't believe me. "There'll be trouble if I catch you again."

I walked away with a sinking heart. I couldn't afford to get into more trouble, so after that, I didn't take anything to the shed. If Molly and Bertie came, I didn't see them.

At Thanksgiving, our church was decorated with golden yellow chrysanthemums that made me think of Edwina and Mrs. Sinclair. I wondered whether the suffragists would soon get the vote for women. Would they make better laws for children's welfare? Molly and Bertie needed help before winter came. Then, as the minister prayed for victory in the war, I thought about Father. We hadn't had a letter from him yet. Mother had said not to worry, that he was too busy to write, but the cold knot in my stomach wouldn't go away. It was there even when I ate roast turkey and when I was tucked into bed at night. I carried my fear for Father everywhere.

One Sunday afternoon, while Bertha snoozed and Mother visited an elderly neighbour lady, I lay in the sprinkle of snow in the backyard, making a snow angel. I hoped that father's guardian angel was with him, wherever he was. Suddenly, something bumped against our high wooden fence. Two hands appeared at the top, then Bertie's face. I jumped up and rushed over.

"Millie," he gasped, "Molly says can yer come 'elp us? We dunno who else ter ask."

"What's the matter?"

"Me little sock and blisters is sick—"

"Who?"

"Ellie and Little Em. An' one cold night, Maw sneaked us into the 'otel to sleep someplace warm. But the guvnor found out an' she were give the boot. No job now."

"Your father—"

"Niver come back to the gates of Rome. We're starvink, Millie. Got anyfink we can nosh on?"

Bertie's face dropped from view as his hands slipped. I climbed up and stared into the alley, where horses' hooves had churned the snow. I was horrified to see that Bertie still had bare feet. He hopped from one foot to the other and his teeth chattered.

"But, Bertie, how did you know where I live?"

"Watched yer come out of school one day. Followed yer back. Please come 'elp, Millie."

"Wait!" I commanded. I dropped down and rushed indoors, my mind racing. I tiptoed into the pantry and shoved food into a paper bag. From my room, I fetched my second-best coat, and from the nursery, I took a baby blanket that Mother never used. From a cabinet, I took a bottle of elixir for fevers and a tin of cough pastilles. Then I rushed outside past my snow angel, hoping it would keep watch over me that afternoon.

"Bertie!" I called softly. "I'm throwing stuff over! Catch!"

I bundled everything inside the blanket and hurled it over the fence. Then I scrambled to the top and dropped into the alley. Bertie had already picked up the bundle.

"We have to get Edwina's mother," I said. "She'll know what to do."

Avoiding patches of ice and frozen horse droppings, we hurried north under the dark, bare trees. Bertie's freckles were faded with cold by the time we climbed Edwina's front steps and banged on the door. Silence. Bertie gave the knocker a tremendous thump. The door opened; I thought the girl standing there must be one of Edwina's big sisters because she had the same blond hair and mischievous blue eyes.

"Is Mrs. Sinclair home?" I panted.

"She's somewhere on College Street, handing out suffragist brochures," the tall girl said, smiling. "Can I help?"

"We'll find 'er!" Bertie hollered, leaping down the steps. Breathlessly, we went south to College Street. Soldiers' boots rang on the frosty ground as they marched past, and the pure notes of a trumpet sounded from the university grounds. Trotting horses breathed plumes of smoke. Bertie wiped his nose on the sleeve of his ragged sweater and whistled tunelessly through his teeth. We had reached Yonge Street and still hadn't found Mrs. Sinclair.

"You'll come anyway, won't yer?" Bertie asked beseechingly as we stood at the corner. "Molly's expectink you."

I remembered the awful slum and shuddered. I didn't want to return there alone; it had been bad enough visiting with Edwina and her mother. I was frightened of the rats, the dark shacks, the rough people with their strange languages and their diseases.

"I can't come. Mother will find out. I have to go home."

Bertie stared at the ground. His toes were as white as dead worms.

"Suit yerself," he said angrily. "Fink yer too good fer us, yeah?"

As he turned, with his eyes hidden below his dirty cap, I saw a tear wet his cheek. I watched him move away, beginning to run with his shoulders hunched over the blanket bundle. I felt terrible, as if I were being torn in two between Bertie's cold hunger and my own fear. Mother didn't know where I was—no one did. What if something happened to me? I thought of the button necklace in my handkerchief drawer at home.

"Bertie, wait!" I cried, beginning to run.

He kept running and so did I, over frozen ruts, past the loud wail of banjos in a tavern, past women who shouted at me and scrawny barking dogs and a black-faced coal man carrying a sack on his bent shoulders. I followed Bertie until he stopped running and we walked on together deeper and deeper into the slum. Finally, we reached his house, leaning into the dirty snow, its walls dark with damp. Bertie shoved the door open and I followed him in. The first room was even barer than before, with only the battered table and the woodstove.

"It's cold!" I shivered. "Is the stove lit?"

"Burnt up the stools. Nofink left to burn but the table. Maw says maybe tomorrer."

"But, Bertie, you need coal!"

"Nofink to buy it with. No bees and honey."

"Where's Molly?"

"Millie?" cried a weak voice, and I followed the sound into the second room. The bed was gone. "Flogged it fer food," said Bertie, noticing my puzzled frown.

Molly lay on the floor among ragged blankets. Her dark hair was a tangled web around her thin face and the blue hollows beneath her eyes. I knelt and saw that the lumps beneath the blankets were her two little sisters. The baby's cheeks were flushed red as she snored in her sleep. Dried mucus smeared her upper lip. Ellie snored with her mouth open.

"Blimey, Millie, yer a sight fer sore eyes," Molly said with the ghost of a smile. Her cold, thin fingers gripped mine tightly.

"I've brought food, Molly," I said. I tried to use the kind of voice my mother used when I was sick. I tried to sound wise and calm, as if nothing bad could happen in the world. Then I added, "I've brought something for fevers. Sit up and help me."

Together, we lifted Little Em and spooned elixir into her mouth; she coughed but then swallowed without opening her eyes. "One teaspoon is enough," I said, reading the label in case Molly couldn't. Molly said she had a sore throat, so I opened the tin of pastilles and everyone sucked one. Then I wrapped Molly in the coat I'd brought, and we wrapped Little Em in the blanket from Louisa May's room. Ellie awoke and sat up. Molly gave her some elixir, too. Ellie began to cry but then stopped when she saw me start to unpack the food.

Sitting on the floor in the freezing house, we had a picnic with the food: the luncheon rolls Bertha had baked, slices of cold roast beef, cheese with a hard red rind, applesauce that everyone slurped straight from the jar. Finally, the food was all gone except for the portion that Molly was saving for their mother. Bertie gathered up the crumbs and licked them from his palms.

"Still got them buttons?" Molly asked and I nodded. She sighed contentedly and lay down beside the little girls. "Yer an Irish stew friend, Millie. Yer the best."

"Where's your mother?"

"Lookin' fer somewhere to swab floors or wash sheets," said Bertie.

"Ain't seen 'er since yesterday," Molly muttered.

I hunched over on the blankets, thinking. Around me, the house sank into its cold, creaking stillness. The air smelled of rot and mould. Faintly, I heard men walk past outside, coughing and spitting. Something rustled in a corner of the kitchen and I turned quickly but saw nothing. There was a dark crack where the door to the addition swung ajar. I shivered. I didn't know what to do for my friends. I was afraid to stay here but just as afraid to leave. The afternoon light faded as I lingered, and the grimy window became dim.

"We should try again to find Mrs. Sin—" I started, but then I saw that everyone in the room had fallen asleep, dishevelled on the heaped blankets.

I felt completely alone.

My stomach cramped with anxiety. I wanted to use the water closet but there wasn't one in this house—only that stinking black hole in the addition, beyond the dark crack. I could not use it.

Leaving the bottle of elixir and tin of pastilles on the dirty bare floor, I crept to the front door. It was colder outside than before, and purple shadows filled the street with strange shapes. I hurried north with my hands in my pockets, staring at the ground and avoiding yellow stains in the trampled snow. A carter cracked his whip and the horses pawed at the slippery surface. A gang of children threw snowballs that hit my shoulders. I rushed past a blind beggar holding out his cap and a woman selling matchsticks on a tray hanging from her neck. "Who's a scared little rabbit?" she said with a guffaw. Her teeth were rotting stumps. Other women walked by in black shawls wrapped over strange bright dresses with embroidered patterns. Their earrings and many bracelets glinted.

My heart beat against my ribs like a hand on a drum.

Then, as I reached the corner of College Street, I glimpsed a woman across the road. I stopped to stare, holding the stitch in my side. It *was* Mrs. Sinclair, with Edwina, handing suffragist brochures to people as they passed. A wave of relief washed through me. Safe; I was safe! Maybe I would even find help for Molly! I dashed out into Yonge Street, calling, "Edwina! Edwina!" in excitement.

The massive wagon hurtled around the corner. Speed blurred its dark shape. Horses' long legs reached for me. Dark shadows threw their net over me. A roar and the clatter of wheels filled

I dashed out into Yonge Street, calling, "Edwina! Edwina!" in excitement. The massive wagon hurtled around the corner.

my brain. My feet froze to the cold slime of the road. I heard Edwina scream and a man's voice shout "Whoa! Whoa!" and Mrs. Sinclair cry "Run, Millie—run!"

Then the horses and the wagon swept into me. Blue sparks filled the air and burst like fireworks. Pain exploded in my body, and everything went black.

CHAPTER Nº 7

My body sagged and bounced with its burden of pain. I wanted to swallow, but my mouth was too dry. Darkness filled my eyes. Were they still closed? I couldn't tell. Only movement was real, the movement of a man walking, carrying my great pain. His boots thumped a rhythm.

"This 'ere's the kitchen door," his voice rumbled into my ear pressed against his chest.

Light touched my eyes but I couldn't see. My lids were too heavy to open and too sticky. I felt myself being lowered onto something soft. Women's voices exclaimed. Warm water touched my face and pain roared in me, like a dragon coming awake.

"Miss Millie, you're safe home," a voice soothed. "Open your eyes, there's a good girl."

A warm cloth gently pressed my forehead, then my eyes. Finally, I opened them, squinting. Bertha's face hovered over me. Beside her stood Bill, our gardener, wearing a soldier's uniform. Mrs. Sinclair and Edwina stood on the other side of the table where I lay on cushions brought from the parlour.

"Where's Mother?" I muttered. My tongue felt swollen.

"Letting the doctor in," said Bertha.

Suddenly, there they were. Mother's face was pinched with anxiety and she still wore her gloves and a bonnet. She held my hand and stroked my hair, looking as though she might cry. Dr. Miller tutted and examined my head.

"Too tough an egg to crack," he joked. "These head cuts aren't very deep although they've bled so much." Then he asked for scissors to cut open my coat sleeve. When he touched my arm, the dragon of pain swallowed me whole and chewed me up. In its stomach, everything was black again.

After that, it was morning—or maybe evening; I can't remember. Light and dark moved across my bedroom walls in strange rhythms. The sheets were hot, then cold. My throat was dry; Mother lifted water to my lips. She sang hymns but when I looked, she had left the room.

Finally, my thoughts cleared. I slid weakly from bed and tottered across the room. In the mirror, my face was pale beneath bandages and my broken arm, heavy in a plaster of Paris cast, hung in a sling. Through the window, I watched Tommy making a snow angel and I looked for the one I'd made. It was still there. Maybe I had not been in bed for years, the way it felt. Molly! Bertie! What had happened to them while I lay in bed? Worry filled my head and I leaned it against the cool glass. I had failed again. I hadn't helped my friends, and Mother would be upset with me, and Father would hear that I'd broken my promise once more. Miserably, I crawled between the sheets and fell into drowsy throbbing pain.

When I awoke, afternoon sun streamed onto the coverlet. A blue jay called. Mother's wedding band and her silver thimble glinted as she sewed beside my bed. She pulled a long strand of blue thread through the fabric bunched in her lap. When she noticed my open eyes, she laid her work down, smoothed my hair away from my bandages, and kissed my cheek.

"Dear Millie," she said softly. "My dear child."

"Mother—" I struggled to sit up and she slid a pillow behind my back. "Mother, you have to help. Please. I know I shouldn't have gone—I know I'm in trouble—but it's Molly and Bertie, and they need help and I didn't know what to do—"

"Hush," Mother soothed. "You're not in trouble. I have heard all about Molly and Bertie. Edwina told me why you both stole the apples. She and her mother guessed why you were alone on Yonge Street when the wagon ran you down. Mrs. Sinclair went to visit Molly's family."

"Are they all right?"

"The children are in foster care now," Mother replied. "They are in a kind, warm home with food and medicine. Mrs. Sinclair is helping their mother find work. It's hard to find a position that pays a woman enough to support a family. But Mrs. Sinclair is a determined woman!"

I sighed and everything tight in me let go. Mrs. Sinclair would not give up until Molly's family was reunited. My friend would be safe now.

"I'm sorry that I didn't know about this sooner," my mother said, sitting down and returning to her sewing. "I would never be cross with you for trying to help others, Millie."

Peacefully, I watched her sew. "Is it something for the soldiers?" I asked.

She laughed. "It is not! It's for a Rosebud."

I sat up from my pillow too suddenly, and my head swam. "Mother!"

"You have been in bed for three days with a concussion," she said. "Mrs. Sinclair and Edwina have come twice every day to see how you fared. Mrs. Sinclair and I have spent considerable time talking. I admire her kind heart. She works tirelessly for what she believes is right. Although I do not agree with all her ideas, I am beginning to see that some of them have great merit. We have agreed it is unnecessary to separate you and Edwina."

"We can be friends again?"

"Yes. It was Edwina who ran to the army encampment and found Bill the night you were struck down. I know she is trustworthy. And I know that I can trust you, Millie, not to go alone into the city any more."

"Yes," I agreed fervently.

"So," continued Mother, "two trustworthy girls should make excellent Rosebuds."

Her smile filled me with warmth. I lay back and thought about tying knots and lighting campfires. Edwina and I would have so much fun in our special Girls Only club!

"Can Edwina come here for tea?" I asked. When Mother nodded, I started planning the fort we would make in the attic and the snowman we'd build outside. Next spring, maybe we'd have a tree house of our own.

The sun slipped across my wall and the blue jay called again. Mother reached for something on my bedside table. "Shall I read this to you?"

"What is it?"

"A letter from Father."

"Oh! Oh, at last!" I reached for the creased envelope with its English stamp and Father's familiar writing: *Mrs. James MacCallum and Miss Millicent MacCallum*. I clutched it tightly, hearing his voice speak my name. Suddenly, he felt much closer to home.

"Is he all right?" I asked.

"He's in better shape than you are," Mother teased. "He's working as an engineer in the shipyards at Tyneside. Many of the men working there are also Scots—one even went to school with Father. So he's not short of company."

I smiled, thinking of how Father loved to laugh and talk, and imagining his broad Scottish brogue.

Mother smiled in return and pulled the letter from the envelope. "*'My dearest Elizabeth, Millie, and Louisa May,'*" she began to read while the sun played in the silver maple outside my window. "*'My loving thoughts are always with you.'*"

Glossary of Cockney Rhyming Slang

Bees and honey: money

China plate: mate (friend)

Davy Crockett: pocket

Gates of Rome: home

Hopping pot: a lot

Irish stew: true

Ones and twos: pair of shoes

Pot and pan: old man (father)

Sock and blisters: sisters

Teapot lid: little kid

Bibliography

TEXT

Bacchi, Carol Lee. *The Ideas of the English-Canadian Suffragists 1877–1918*. Toronto: University of Toronto Press, 1983.

Bercham, F. R. *Opportunity Road: Yonge Street 1860–1939*. Toronto: Natural Heritage Press, 1996.

Boothman, Lucy Martyn. *Toronto: 100 Years of Grandeur*. Toronto: Pagurian Press, 1984.

Cleverdon, Catherine L. *The Woman Suffrage Movement in Canada* (2nd ed.). Toronto: University of Toronto Press, 1974.

Hall, Roger, and Dodds, Gordon. *Ontario 200 Years in Pictures*. Toronto: Dundurn Press, 1991.

West, Bruce. *Toronto*. Toronto: Doubleday, 1967.

WEB

Children's Aid Society of Toronto, *Annual Report 1907*, Toronto Archives. Available online at http://ohq.tpl.toronto.on.ca. Accessed February 15, 2005.

Civic Survey Committee 1913, City of Toronto Archives, Ontario History Quest. Available online at http://ohq.tpl.toronto.on.ca. Accessed February 15, 2005.

"History of Child Welfare in Ontario," Ontario Association of Children's Aid Societies. Available online at www.oacas.org/resources/history.htm. Accessed February 15, 2005.

"History of Guiding," Girl Guides of Ontario. Available online at www.guidesontario.org/about us/ghistory.htm. Accessed February 15, 2005.

"Toronto Archives Image Database," City of Toronto Archives. Available online at www.city.toronto.on.ca/archives/photographs. Accessed February 15, 2005.

Dear Reader,

Welcome back to the continuing adventures of Our Canadian Girl! It's been another exciting year for us here at Penguin, publishing new stories and continuing the adventures of twelve terrific girls. The best part of this past year, though, has been the wonderful letters we've received from readers like you, telling us about your favourite Our Canadian Girl story, and the parts you liked the most. Best of all, you told us which stories you would like to read, and we were amazed! There are so many remarkable stories in Canadian history. It seems that wherever we live, great stories live too, in our towns and cities, on our rivers and mountains. Thank you so much for sharing them.

So please, stay in touch. Write letters, log on to our website (www.ourcanadiangirl.ca), let us know what you think of Our Canadian Girl. We're listening.

Sincerely,
Barbara Berson

Canada's

1608
Samuel de Champlain establishes the first fortified trading post at Quebec.

1755
The British expel the entire French population of Acadia (today's Maritime provinces), sending them into exile.

1759
The British defeat the French in the Battle of the Plains of Abraham.

1776
The 13 Colonies revolt against Britain, and the Loyalists flee to Canada.

1784
Rachel

1812
The United States declares war against Canada.

1837
Calling for responsible government, the Patriotes, following Louis-Joseph Papineau, rebel in Lower Canada; William Lyon Mackenzie leads the uprising in Upper Canada.

1845
The expedition of Sir John Franklin to the Arctic ends when the ship is frozen in the pack ice; the fate of its crew remains a mystery.

1867
New Brunswick, Nova Scotia and the United Province of Canada come together in Confederation to form the Dominion of Canada.

1869
Louis Riel leads his Métis followers in the Red River Rebellion.

1870
Manitoba joins Canada. The Northwest Territories become an official territory of Canada.

1871
British Columbia joins Canada.

Timeline

1873
Prince Edward Island joins Canada.

1885
At Craigellachie, British Columbia, the last spike is driven to complete the building of the Canadian Pacific Railway.

1896
Gold is discovered on Bonanza Creek, a tributary of the Klondike River.

1898
The Yukon Territory becomes an official territory of Canada.

1905
Alberta and Saskatchewan join Canada.

1914
Britain declares war on Germany, and Canada, because of its ties to Britain, is at war too.

1917
In the Halifax harbour, two ships collide, causing an explosion that leaves more than 1,600 dead and 9,000 injured.

1918
As a result of the Wartime Elections Act, the women of Canada are given the right to vote in federal elections.

1939
Canada declares war on Germany seven days after war is declared by Britain and France.

1945
World War II ends conclusively with the dropping of atomic bombs on Hiroshima and Nagasaki.

1949
Newfoundland, under the leadership of Joey Smallwood, joins Canada.

1885
Marie-Claire

1902
Keeley

1914
Millie